Dedicated to Megan Lynn Troglen, a wonderful
child and great horse lover. —M.D.

For Geeta Morris and her family. —L.M.

Published by Greenleaf Book Group Press
Austin, Texas
www.gbgpress.com

Distributed by Greenleaf Book Group LLC

For ordering information or special discounts for bulk purchases, please contact
Greenleaf Book Group LLC at PO Box 91869, Austin, TX 78709, 512.891.6100.

Design and composition by Greenleaf Book Group LLC
Cover design by Greenleaf Book Group LLC
Illustrations by Lyn Martin

Cataloging-in-Publication data (Prepared by The Donohue Group, Inc.)

DeLand, M. Maitland.

Busy bees at work and play / M. Maitland DeLand ; with illustrations by Lyn Martin. -- 1st ed.

p. : ill. ; cm.

Summary: A mother bee shows her child how different types of workers help the
community while reinforcing that there is a time for work and a time for play.

Interest age level: 3-5.

ISBN: 978-1-60832-028-8

1. Bees--Juvenile fiction. 2. Occupations--Juvenile fiction. 3. Work--Juvenile fiction. 4. Play--Juvenile fiction.
5. Bees--Fiction. 6. Occupations--Fiction. 7. Work--Fiction. 8. Play--Fiction. I. Martin, J. Lyn. II. Title.

PZ7.D37314 Bu 2010

[E]

Part of the Tree Neutral™ program, which offsets the number of trees consumed in
the production and printing of this book by taking proactive steps, such as planting
trees in direct proportion to the number of trees used: www.treeneutral.com.

TreeNeutral™

Manufactured by Shanghai iPrinting Co., Ltd on acid-free paper
Manufactured in Shanghai, China. December 2009
Batch No. 1

09 10 11 12 13 14   10 9 8 7 6 5 4 3 2 1

First Edition

Busy Bees
AT Work AND Play

M. Maitland DeLand
with illustrations by Lyn Martin

GREENLEAF
BOOK GROUP PRESS

Mama Bee was headed out of the house,

When Bambina Bee grabbed the sleeve of her blouse.

"Momma, why do you have to work today?

Why can't you stay home and play?"

"My little Bambina, throughout the day,
There's a time for work and a time for play.

Walk around our town and you will see,
How working helps our community."

Letter Carrier Bee delivers the mail.
Aunt Bee sent Sue Bee a shovel and pail.

And when work is done at the end of the day,
How does Letter Carrier Bee like to play?

Plumber Bee fixes pipes that bring us all water
So Jan Bee can give a drink to her baby bee daughter.

And when work is done at the end of the day,
How does Plumber Bee like to play?

Doctor Bee examines and mends you and me.
She's putting a bandage on Bonnie Bee's knee.

And when work is done at the end of the day,
How does Doctor Bee like to play?

Ferryboat Bee sails to the far shore.

She lets passengers off, then picks up some more.

And when work is done at the end of the day,

How does Ferryboat Bee like to play?

Chef Bee cooks meals that are fit for a queen. For Donna Bee, he grilled the biggest burger she's ever seen.

And when work is done at the end of the day, How does Chef Bee like to play?

Computer Bee fixes the cables and cords

So Ben Bee can reach the computer keyboard.

And when work is done at the end of the day,

How does Computer Bee like to play?

Farmer Bee grows crops that we eat with pleasure.

She gives Sasha Bee peaches in the hot summer weather.

And when work is done at the end of the day,
How does Farmer Bee like to play?

Policeman Bee makes sure that we all live in safety.

He slows down Bobby Bee when he is too hasty.

And when work is done at the end of the day,
How does Policeman Bee like to play?

Bus Driver Bee takes us all over town.

The playground is where Sammy Bee steps down.

And when work is done at the end of the day,
How does Bus Driver Bee like to play?

Zookeeper Bee keeps the animals happy.

Barney Bee thinks that the turtles look snappy.

And when work is done at the end of the day,
How does Zookeeper Bee like to play?

Carpenter Bee helps us build our buildings.

He made Lee Bee a playhouse, isn't that thrilling?

And when work is done at the end of the day,
How does Carpenter Bee like to play?

Fireman Bee helps us whenever there's trouble.

To save Billy Bee's cat, he arrived on the double.

And when work is done at the end of the day,
How does Fireman Bee like to play?

I am a teacher, and I help bees learn
About planets and monkeys and why fires burn.

Come on now, Bambina, it's time to play.
Our town has declared a holiday!

Bambina Bee said, "Momma, I want to work, too."

"You work hard, my Bambina, just being you."